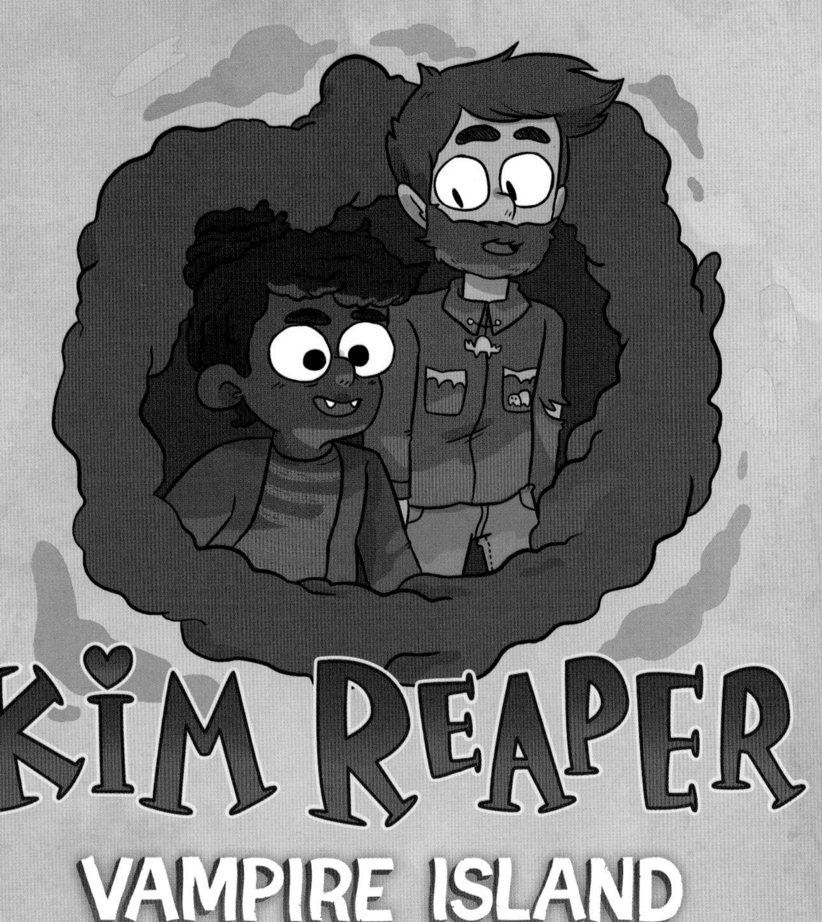

KiM REAPER

VAMPIRE ISLAND

AN ONI PRESS PUBLICATION

VAMPIRE ISLAND

BY SARAH GRALEY

COLOR ASSISTS BY STEF PURENINS

LETTERED BY CRANK!

Designed by Hilary Thompson & Kate Z. Stone
Edited by Ari Yarwood

PUBLISHED BY ONI PRESS, INC.

Joe Nozemack, founder & chief financial officer
James Lucas Jones, publisher
Sarah Gaydos, editor in chief
Charlie Chu, v.p. of creative & business development
Brad Rooks, director of operations
Melissa Meszaros, director of publicity
Margot Wood, director of sales
Sandy Tanaka, marketing design manager
Amber O'Neill, special projects manager
Troy Look, director of design & production
Kate Z. Stone, senior graphic designer
Sonja Synak, graphic designer
Angie Knowles, digital prepress lead
Robin Herrera, senior editor
Ari Yarwood, senior editor
Desiree Wilson, associate editor
Kate Light, editorial assistant
Michelle Nguyen, executive assistant
Jung Lee, logistics coordinator

Originally published as issues 1-4 of the Oni Press comic series Kim Reaper: Vampire Island

ONIPRESS.COM
FACEBOOK.COM/ONIPRESS
TWITTER.COM/ONIPRESS
ONIPRESS.TUMBLR.COM
INSTAGRAM.COM/ONIPRESS

SARAHGRALEY.COM
FACEBOOK.COM/SARAHGRALEYART
TWITTER.COM/SARAHGRALEYART
SARAHSSKETCHBOOK.TUMBLR.COM
INSTAGRAM.COM/SARAHGRALEY

First Edition: June 2019
ISBN: 978-1-62010-637-2
eISBN: 978-1-62010-639-6
Convention Exclusive ISBN: 978-1-62010-638-9

1 2 3 4 5 6 7 8 9 10

Library of Congress Control Number: 2018964747

Printed in China.

CHAPTER ONE

I COULD PORTAL TO HER ROOM--SHE KNOWS WE'RE SUPPOSED TO HANG OUT TONIGHT, RIGHT? OR--

MAYBE SHE'S NOT ANSWERING THE DOOR BECAUSE SHE'S IN ***DANGER?!***

SHE'S REALLY GOOD AT TEXTING BACK! SOMETHING MUST BE WRONG!!

FINALLY, I HAVE YOU... AFTER MONTHS OF PURSUIT, YOU'RE FINALLY MINE.
RIP
RIP

THERE'S NO ESCAPE...

...THERE'S NO GOING BACK!!
AAAAAH!!

BECKA!!
AAAAAAAAAAAH!!!
KIM!

WHY AREN'T YOU PICKING UP YOUR PHONE? I'VE BEEN KNOCKING ON YOUR DOOR FOR AGES!

...ACTUALLY, SCRATCH THAT. WHAT IS *UH*, WHAT'S ALL THIS?
EXCUSE ME? ALL THIS?

IT'S ONLY THE HOTTEST SHOW ON RIGHT NOW. IT COMBINES THE COMPLEXITIES OF BEAUTIFUL AND MACABRE VAMPIRES WITH THE DRAMA OF TEENAGE LIFE.

"YOU KNOW THOSE BONEHEADS STUCK ME WITH THE WORST HOURS SINCE I BROKE THE RULES. I JUST WISH THERE WAS SOMETHING I COULD DO ABOUT IT..."
I'M SO TIRED!!
SO TIRED MY EYES ARE PLAYING TRICKS ON ME. YOU'RE NOT WEARING COSTUMES... ARE YOU?
I'M A CUTE DRACULA!!
IT HEIGHTENS THE VIEWING EXPERIENCE.
WELL, I THINK THIS SHOW IS AN INCREDIBLY FLATTERING TAKE ON VAMPIRES.
REAL VAMPIRES ARE FAR MORE RIDICULOUS, IN MY OPINION. THEY THINK THEY'RE SO COOL, IN THEIR BIG CLASSY CASTLE, ON THEIR BIG FANCY ISLAND, BUT LET ME TELL YOU--
THEY'RE NOT!!

NOT A BIG FAN OF VAMPIRES, KIM?
HMMMMMM.
WHOAWHOAWHOA, MORE IMPORTANTLY, KIM...
...ARE VAMPIRES REAL? AND THEY LIVE IN A CASTLE? ON AN ISLAND?!
ON A VAMPIRE ISLAND?!
...MAYBE.
AAAAAAAAAH!!
WHAT ELSE EXISTS? WHY DIDN'T YOU TELL ME EARLIER? HOW DO YOU KNOW?!
WELL...
...I GUESS IT NEVER REALLY CAME UP.
I HAVE TO KNOW ABOUT ALL THE MONSTERS OUT THERE, WITH SOULS, AT LEAST.
IT'S PART OF MY JOB!
WHAT, UH, WHAT ARE YOU DOING?
OH, MY, GOSH...
...LET'S GO TO VAMPIRE ISLAND!!
UH OH.

C'MON, LET'S GO ON AN ADVENTURE! I WANNA HANG OUT IN A CASTLE, KIM! I WANNA HANG OUT ON VAMPIRE ISLAND WITH YOU!!
I DON'T KNOW...
CAN... I COME TOO?
YEAH, I SUPER DON'T KNOW ABOUT THAT.
I NEED TO MAKE SURE BECKA STAYS SAFE, BECAUSE SHE'S MY FRIEND.
BUT ALSO, I NEED SOMEONE TO WATCH SEASON TWO OF *VAMPIRE TEEN DRAMA* WITH ME.
TYLER GOT ME INTO VAMPIRES, SO IT ONLY MAKES SENSE HE COMES TOO!
AH, SO HE'S RESPONSIBLE FOR THIS.
ARE YOU SURE YOU WANT TO GO ON A DATE WITH TYLER IN TOW TO AN ISLAND OF VAMPIRES?
YEAH!
OKAY, SOME RULES.
RULE ONE! NON-VAMPIRES ARE NOT ALLOWED ON VAMPIRE ISLAND. IF ANYONE ASKS, YOU JUST CAN'T GET ENOUGH OF THE RED STUFF.
RULE TWO! TAKE OFF THOSE GOOFY CLOAKS, THOSE ARE SO LAST CENTURY VAMPIRE FASHION. LUCKILY ***SCARVES*** ARE IN, BECAUSE WE NEED TO KEEP THOSE UN-BITTEN NECKS COVERED AT ALL TIMES.
RULE THREE! I'M A REALLY COOL DUDE. ***ADMIT IT, TYLER!***
NO.
TYLER, I WANNA SEE THE VAMPIRES!!
FINE... YOU ARE... PRETTY OKAY.
NICE.
RIGHT, FOLLOW ME TO THE WEIRDEST DATE OF ALL TIME!
YAAAY!

READY YOUR FOOTING, GANG, WE'RE ABOUT TO ARRIVE!
H-HOW DO YOU--
HEY, CAREFUL THERE! IF YOU GET ANY SCRAPES OR CUTS, I'M OPENING THAT PORTAL BACK UP.
ACK!
C'MON TYLER, WE DIDN'T GET DRESSED UP FOR NOTHING!!
WE DIDN'T GET DRESSED UP AT ALL.
I DON'T KNOW ABOUT THAT, THESE SCARVES ARE QUITE FANCY.
GOOD EVENING, WE'RE HERE FOR THE, *UH,* VAMPIRE STUFF? Y'ALL HAVING A PARTY? FOR VAMPIRES-- LIKE US?
YOU GUYS READY TO PARTY, GHOUL STYLE?
EEEEEEEEE!

YOU'LL HAVE TO EXCUSE THEM, THEY'RE NEW BLOOD.
I MEAN, NO BLOOD! WHATSOEVER!!
I ONLY JUST BIT THEM LAST WEEK, HA HA. YOU KNOW HOW IT IS!
VAMPIRES ARE NO FUN.
HEY, YOU PROBABLY DON'T WANT TO DRINK THAT--
IT'S PROBABLY BLOOD.
BLEEEEEUUUGH!!

SO, *UH*, HOW'S BEING IN A NERD CASTLE GOING FOR YOU GUYS? HAVING FUN?
WHAT?

I WISH YOU'D GOT HOOKED ON A SHOW WHERE PEOPLE DRINK OUT OF PINEAPPLES, INSTEAD OF NECKS--
LOOK, IT GETS REALLY GOOD WHEN THEY INTRODUCE THE HOT VAMPIRE TWINS!

YOU THINK YOU'RE TOO COOL FOR TV!
I'M SORRY, I'M TOO BUSY FOR ***BAD TV!*** I'M ALWAYS WORKING!!
UM, YOU GUYS...
THERE'S A WEIRD PERSON WATCHING US...

GUYS?

TYLER HAD TO GO... TO THE OTHER SIDE OF THE ROOM. WE, *UHHH*, HAD A DISAGREEANCE.
DID YOU SEE THE CREEPER ON THE BALCONY?

THEY WERE PROBABLY SCOPING YOU OUT-- YOU ***ARE*** THE CUTEST DRACULA, AFTER ALL.
AWH, KIM, I'M SERIOUS. THEY WERE REALLY SPOOKY!

ANYWHERE WITH YOU IS SOMEWHERE I WANT TO BE.

I ***PROMISE*** WE CAN GO SOMEWHERE QUIET LIKE THE CINEMA NEXT TIME, I JUST REALLY FANCIED AN ADVENTURE DATE, Y'KNOW?

HE'S MY BEST FRIEND, KIM! I WANT HIM TO BE YOUR FRIEND, TOO!

HE LISTENS TO MY PROBLEMS! HE LIKES THE SAME PIZZA I DO! HE LIKES BOARD GAMES DESPITE THE LONG SET-UP--HE PAYS HIS RENT ON TIME *AND* HE'S A TIDY HOUSEMATE, KIM!

HE'S A COOL GUY!

HIM?

I'LL TRY FOR YOU, BUT I'M MAKING NO PROMISES.
THAT'S ALL I WANT! I'LL FEEL AT EASE KNOWING IF YOU'VE TRIED, BUT YOU'RE PROBABLY DESTINED TO BE PALS. I HAVE GOOD TASTE IN FRIENDS!!

UMM... THAT'S NOT WHAT I THINK IT IS, IS IT?
I'M SUPPOSED TO HAVE THE EVENING OFF...

KIM! COME TO WORK ASAP, WE NEED YOU TO FILL A LAST MINUTE SHIFT.
I GUESS ME AND TYLER WILL HAVE TO BECOME BFFS LATER.
NOOOOO!

THIS NEEDS TO STOP HAPPENING. THIS IS WHY I DON'T WANT TO GO ON CINEMA DATES--YOU'D HAVE TO LEAVE MID-FILM!
I'LL BE BACK REAL QUICK, I SWEAR!
JUST REMEMBER-- IF ANYONE ASKS, BITING IS, LIKE, YOUR NUMBER ONE HOBBY.
HEY, DID YOU HEAR THIS GUY'S JOKE?!
W-WHA?
TELL IT AGAIN!
YEAH!
UM, OKAY...
DO YOU GUYS HAVE ANY FOOD THAT'S, UM...
BWAAAHAHAHA!
...VEGAN?

WHAT A WEIRD JOKE FOR A VAMPIRE TO MAKE...

I MET HIM AT THE DOOR! HE'S NEW *BLOOD!*

BWAHAHAHAHAH!

BECKA! THANK GOSH YOU'RE HERE-- WHERE'S KIM?

I UNDERSTAND HER APATHY TOWARDS VAMPIRES NOW, AND I'D REALLY LIKE TO GO HOME, WHERE VAMPIRES ARE ONLY ON THE SCREEN.
YEAH, UM, SHE HAD TO NIP OUT FOR A BIT, SO IT'S JUST YOU AND ME, BUDDY.

LOOK, LET'S JUST TAKE A BREATHER TO THE SIDE AND MAYBE NOT DRAW ANY MORE ATTENTION TO OURSELVES WHILE WE'RE STUCK HERE.
THERE WERE VEGAN VAMPIRES IN *VAMPIRE TEEN DRAMA!!*

ACK!! STUPID CHAIR!!

WHY IS ALL VAMPIRE FURNITURE POINTY, OR COVERED IN SPIKES? WHAT KIND OF AESTHETIC IS THAT, REALLY?! NOT A COMFY ONE, *THAT'S* FOR SURE--
TYLER...!

OH NO, THAT'S A DEEP CUT!
WHAT AM I GOING TO DO?! WHAT AM I GOING TO--
BECKA?
THAT'S A TIGHT KNOT, AND SHOULD SLOW THE BLEEDING.
BUT WHAT ABOUT--
YOUR ARM IS MUCH MORE IMPORTANT THAN THAT SCARF, YOU BLOODY IT UP ALL YOU LIKE, PAL!
NO, I MEAN--
OH! OH... I FORGOT ABOUT THAT.
THAT ONE'S GUSHING BLOOD! BLOOD!
THAT ONE HAS NO NECK BITES!!
I THINK WE MIGHT HAVE SOME PARTY CRASHERS.
SOME BLOODY, UNWANTED GUESTS...
SO, UH, WHEN'S KIM COMING BACK WITH THAT BEAUTIFUL PORTAL STICK OF HERS?

I'M NOT SURE, SO IT LOOKS LIKE WE'RE GONNA HAVE TO TAKE MATTERS INTO OUR OWN HANDS AND, *UH--*
RUN!!
DIDN'T YOU TAKE ON A HORDE OF ZOMBIES BY YOURSELF THAT ONE TIME?
THIS IS DIFFERENT!! I HAD A ROLLING PIN, AND ZOMBIES CAN'T FLY! FLYING ENEMIES ARE HARDER TO HIT AND ABOUT A MILLION TIMES MORE ***SCARY!***
I FORGOT ABOUT YOUR BIRD-PHOBIA.
I AM SO NOT AFRAID OF BIRDS.
SO, *UH*, IS THIS HOW ALL YOUR DATES GO WITH KIM? ROMANCE WITH AN INCREDIBLE SENSE OF PERIL?
STOP IT, TYLER!!

I REALLY WISH YOU'D GIVE HER A CHANCE! IT FEELS LIKE YOU'VE ALREADY WRITTEN HER OFF!

BAF!

SHE MAKES ME HAPPY!
BECKA...

ACK! DEAD END!
NOT QUITE! LET'S HIDE IN HERE!!

LOOK... I GUESS I'VE BEEN HARSH ON KIM, BUT IT'S ONLY BECAUSE I WORRY ABOUT YOU. I WANT YOU TO STAY SAFE!
SHE'S A GRIM REAPER... YOUR EX THAT WORKED AT THAT RECORD STORE WAS A LOT MORE, UH, CHILL? MILD? NOT A PART-TIME ANGEL OF DEATH?
THEY WERE ONLY DATING ME TO GET TO YOU, THOUGH!

...

FINE, I'LL GIVE KIM A CHANCE IF WE SURVIVE THIS, OKAY?
GOOD!

ON THAT NOTE, WHAT IS THE SURVIVAL PLAN?
WE GOT THE LEAD ON THOSE VAMPIRES, AND A HEAVY DOOR BETWEEN US NOW. LET'S BARRICADE THIS AND WAIT IT OUT!
SERIOUSLY?

KIM'S GOTTA BE BACK SOON, AND WHEN SHE IS, SHE'LL WHISK US AWAY TO SAFETY!
BUT WHAT HAPPENS IF SHE'S NOT?

THIS IS TOTALLY UNFAIR, AND YOU KNOW IT!! YOU'VE BEEN GIVING ME ALL THE WORST JOBS, AND NOW THIS--
YOU CAN'T TALK TO ME LIKE THAT, I'M YOUR SUPERIOR!

YOU MADE ME REAP ALL THOSE PUPPY SOULS, WHICH WAS THE ***SADDEST JOB SO FAR***, AND YOU KNOW IT!

BUT NOW YOU WANT ME TO DO YOUR LAUNDRY?! THAT'S NOT PART OF MY JOB DESCRIPTION! WHAT GIVES?!

IT BECAME PART OF YOUR JOB DESCRIPTION WHEN YOU BROKE THE RULES!
NOW WASH MY BOXERS, I NEED A CLEAN PAIR FOR TOMORROW.
AAAAARGH!

MAYBE WE SHOULD ALSO HIDE? JUST IN CASE?!
I'M A FAN OF THAT PLAN.

I'M, UH, I'M STARTING TO REALLY FREAK OUT NOW, TO BE HONEST.
WE'LL JUST HIDE IN THIS CUPBOARD AND IT'LL ALL BLOW OVER SHORTLY, I PROMISE!!
SOON WE'LL BE BACK HOME, WATCHING VAMPIRE TEEN DRAMA AND--
YEAH NO, I THINK I'M ALL VAMPIRED OUT, ACTUALLY.
BUT THERE'S ONLY TWO MORE EPISODES OF--
SSSHHH!
BOMF
BOMF
BOMF
I'VE FOUND DINNER, BOYS!
THIS IS NOT WHAT I WANT ON MY TOMBSTONE!!
IT'S NOT OVER YET.
RIP
ME
I'VE GOT A NEW PLAN.

ARE YOU READY FOR THIS, HUMAN?
I DUNNO, YOU TELL ME--
THWACK
ROLLING PIN: +3 ATTACK
WHAT THE HECK, BECKA?!
LOOK WHAT I FOUND IN THAT CABINET! LOOKS LIKE I'M NOT GOING DOWN WITHOUT A FIGHT-- WHO'S NEXT?!
ME.

WHAT IS HAPPENING?!

IN EPISODE THREE OF *VAMPIRE TEEN DRAMA*, WILSON TRANSFORMS INTO A BAT TO STEAL TOBY'S DIARY... I THINK THIS IS A STAPLE VAMPIRE ABILITY!

WHOA!!

THE VAMPIRE TOLD ME TO TRUST THEM, WHAT DO YOU RECKON?

I RECKON YOU SHOULD BASH THEM OVER THE HEAD WITH THE ROLLING PIN.

HMMMMM!

THEY'RE TOO TALL, I CAN'T REACH--

AAAAAAAAAAH!!

STOP STRUGGLING, I'M TRYING TO RESCUE YOU!!

WHY WERE YOU WATCHING US EARLIER?
HEADS UP, WE'VE GOT COMPANY.
WHY ARE YOU HELPING US?!
BECAUSE A FRIEND OF KIM'S IS A FRIEND OF MINE.

CHAPTER TWO

THIS ISN'T NORMAL, RIGHT?!
BEING CHASED BY VAMPIRES? NO, NOT REALLY.

I MEAN, I DID GET POSSESSED BY GHOULS PRETTY RECENTLY...

MAYBE THIS IS MY "NORMAL" NOW!
W-WHAT?!

I DO NOT LIKE KIM REAPER!

YOU SAID YOU WERE GONNA GIVE HER A CHANCE!
THAT WAS BEFORE THE GHOUL NEWS!!

HEY, UH--
SORRY TO
INTERRUPT...
OH!
WHAT'S,
UH, WHAT'S
UP?

WE'RE GONNA HIDE
OUT IN THIS ROOM
UP AHEAD, SO I'M
JUST GONNA SWADDLE
YOU GUYS FOR THE
LANDING... LIKE, NOT
IN A WEIRD WAY.
THAT OKAY?
SOUNDS
GREAT.
FOR
SURE.

I FORGOT
THAT WE
WERE BEING
CARRIED.
SSSHH!
READY
YOURSELVES...
OOOH.
T-THANKS...!

NOW QUICK, HELP ME
BLOCK THE DOOR!! WE SHOULD
BE SAFE IN HERE FOR NOW,
AS LONG AS WE BUILD A
GOOD BARRICADE.
OKAY!
CRAFT
CRAFT ROO
GLITTER

HEY, TYLER, QUICK SIDEBAR--

NO TIME FOR SIDEBARS! GET BLOCKING!!
EEP!

BECKA, C'MERE! HELP ME MOVE THIS CABINET.
SURE THING!!

WHY AREN'T YOU HELPING OUT?
WHAT'S YOUR READ ON OUR NEW TOOTHY FRIEND?

WE'RE BLOCKING THE OTHER VAMPIRES OUT... BUT WE'RE ALSO TRAPPING OURSELVES IN WITH THIS FANGY STRANGER!
CAN WE TRUST THEM? WHAT IF THIS IS A TRAP?!

WELL, THEY WERE QUITE SCARY AS A LARGE BAT.

BUT NOW THEY SEEM PRETTY OKAY...

I SUPPOSE MY READ ON THIS VAMPIRE IS THAT WE'VE ALREADY SEALED THE DOOR SO THERE'S NO GOING BACK!

CRAFT
I'M SURE THEY'RE FINE-- THEY *ARE*, RIGHT?
KIM APPARENTLY KNOWS THEM, SO THAT'S SOMETHING... I JUST NEED TO KNOW MORE, THOUGH.
I'D FEEL SAFER.
WELL, KIM WILL BE BACK WITH HER PORTAL STICK ANY TIME NOW!

AS LONG AS WE KEEP OUR DISTANCE AND WAIT THIS OUT, WE'LL MAKE IT OUT OF HERE SAFE AND SOUND!
YEAH!

AAAAH!

AW, JEEZ, I'M SORRY IF I SPOOKED YOU.

AS I AM QUITE A SPOOKY ENTITY, IT CAN BE UNAVOIDABLE!

BUT I PROMISE, YOU WON'T BE AROUND TO BE SPOOKED FOR MUCH LONGER...

HEY! PUT THOSE TEETH AWAY, BOZO, AND BACK OFF!!
W-WHAT?

NO! NO! YOU THOUGHT I WAS GOING TO EAT YOU?! I-I'M TOTALLY OFFENDED!!

OH, JEEZ, BECKA...
CAN'T JUST ASSUME A VAMPIRE IS GONNA EAT YOU, THOUGH...
TYLER!! WE'RE ON THE SAME TEAM!

IN BECKA'S DEFENSE, THE WORDING YOU USED WASN'T GREAT.
THANK YOU. YEAH, PAL, WHAT DID YOU MEAN WE'RE NOT GOING TO BE AROUND MUCH LONGER?

WELL, I SAID I'D HELP YOU--I'VE ALREADY SET THE RESCUE MISSION IN MOTION!
OOOOOOOH.

SO... DO YOU WANT TO HEAR THE PLAN? IT'S REALLY GOOD, AND COMES AT GREAT SACRIFICE TO MYSELF!
AWWW, THAT'S SWEET OF YOU.
UM, SURE.
FIRST UP, I MADE A PHONE CALL ON THE LAND LINE, ALSO KNOWN AS THE RUBBISH OLD-TIMEY PHONE. THEY'RE OUTDATED, JUST LIKE VAMPIRES, AND THAT'S WHY WE HAVE THESE IN THE CASTLE. YOU WANT TO ORDER TAKEAWAY? NO INTERNET, YOU'LL HAVE TO MAKE AN AWKWARD PHONE CALL. MY FIRST SACRIFICE!!
THEN I PLACED AN ORDER FOR ONE HUNDRED GARLIC PIZZAS. ONE HUNDRED. THAT'S MY SECOND SACRIFICE--MY REPUTATION WITH THE ONLY PIZZA PLACE IN TOWN. THE GROSSEST PIZZA, BUT IT'LL KNOCK OUT EVERY VAMPIRE IN THE CASTLE! YOU'LL BE ABLE TO MAKE YOUR GETAWAY!
BUT THAT'S MY THIRD SACRIFICE... I'LL ALSO BE KNOCKED OUT, AND ONCE EVERYONE COMES TO, THEY'LL WANT ME EVEN MORE DEAD THAN I ALREADY AM!

I SAID I'D HELP YOU ESCAPE BECAUSE OF KIM, AND THAT'S TRUE, BUT...
...*I* NEED ***YOUR*** HELP ESCAPING, TOO!!

WE WANT TO HELP YOU...

...BUT WE NEED TO KNOW MORE FIRST!! WHAT HAPPENS AFTER WE BREAK YOU OUT?

WILL VAMPIRES HUNT YOU DOWN--HUNT ***US*** DOWN?!
HOW DO YOU KNOW KIM--

--WHO ARE YOU?!

CHARLIE?

KIM...!

YOU LEFT THE PARTY BEFORE I COULD SAY ANYTHING--
ALL THIS TIME... I THOUGHT YOU WERE DEAD?

I MEAN... I KIND OF AM! I'M UNDEAD, I SUPPOSE--

YOU'RE ALIVE!
I--I MISSED YOU SO MUCH.

HEY, YOU OKAY?
UM, YEAH... YEAH, I'M FINE.

SO, KIIIIM, DO YOU WANT TO INTRODUCE US TO YOUR LONG-LOST FRIEND THERE? CHARLIE, WAS IT?

INTRODUCTIONS! OF COURSE!!

THIS IS MY GIRLFRIEND, BECKA, AND HER ANNOYING HOUSEMATE, TYLER--
HEY!
UM, HI.

BECKA, THIS IS MY BEST FRIEND, CHARLIE!

B-BEST FRIEND?
HEY, I KNOW THAT LOOK. C'MON NOW.

I'M NOT JEALOUS, TYLER! LIKE, KIM CAN HAVE, LIKE, BEST FRIENDS.
THAT AREN'T ME!
IT'S TOTALLY COOL, I'M COOL!

OKAY FINE, I AM TOTALLY UNCOOL! I WANT TO BE COOL, BUT IT'S HARD!!
BECKA...

KIM THOUGHT CHARLIE WAS DEAD, SO THIS IS A BIG DEAL... JUST 'COS THEY'RE BESTIES DOESN'T MEAN ANYTHING MORE.
WE'RE BESTIES, AND KIM IS OKAY WITH THAT.
CHARLIE MIGHT EVEN THINK KIM IS UGLY AS HELL, YOU JUST DON'T KNOW!
SO YOU SHOULDN'T WORRY ABOUT IT.
TYLER!!
SO, HOW DO YOU, UH--HOW DO YOU GUYS KNOW EACH OTHER THEN? YOU, UH, THOUGHT THEY WERE DEAD FOR A BIT? THAT SOUNDS FUN!
UM, NOT REALLY.
ME AND CHARLIE GO WAY BACK! HEY, HELP ME OUT WITH THIS, YEAH?
AW, LOOK, THAT'S ME BEFORE I GOT MY FANGS!
YOU GUYS READY FOR A BACKSTORY?
ALWAYS.

ONCE UPON A TIME, CHARLIE AND I WERE MORTAL AS HELL.
I WAS A "VAMPIRE HUNTER," AND KIM WAS A GOOD FRIEND WHO HUMOURED ME.
WANTED
I DIDN'T REALLY BELIEVE IN VAMPIRES, BUT... I JUST WANTED AN EXCUSE TO HANG WITH KIM.
DUDE!!
THERE WASN'T MUCH ELSE TO DO BEING A TEEN, APART FROM "HUNTING VAMPIRES" IN A SLEEPY TOWN!
THE EGG ON MY FACE NOW, OH JEEZ!
"WE'D HANG OUT IN THE WOODS AT NIGHT ALL THE TIME, LOOKING FOR VAMPIRES--

"WE NEVER THOUGHT WE'D ACTUALLY FIND ANY...
CRACK
"...OR THAT THEY WOULD FIND US
HISSSSSS

WE GOT SPLIT UP IN THE HYSTERIA... I DON'T KNOW YOUR PART OF THE STORY, CHARLIE.
YOU CAN GUESS...

"IT WAS SO DARK OUT... ONE MOMENT YOU WERE NEXT TO ME, THE NEXT--

"--I WAS ALL ALONE.
"OR SO I THOUGHT...

"I TOOK A BREATHER. I STOPPED FOR A MINUTE AND TRIED TO COLLECT MY THOUGHTS.

"THAT'S ALL THEY NEEDED. IT HAPPENED SO FAST..."

BUT ENOUGH ABOUT ME!!
WHAT HAPPENED TO YOU?

OH, CHARLIE...
I'LL GET OVER IT. I MEAN, I'LL LIVE FOREVER. I'LL HAVE FOREVER TO GET OVER THIS.
I'M JUST SO HAPPY YOU GOT AWAY!
WELL, I SORT OF DID...
IT WAS A WET NIGHT.
"I SLIPPED.
"AND I FELL. I FELL REAL HARD.
"I HIT MY HEAD EVEN HARDER.

"AND THAT'S WHEN I FIRST MET HIM.

"MY FIRST ENCOUNTER WITH *DEATH*."

W-WHAT ARE YOU DOING??

"MY CURRENT EMPLOYER."

M-ME?
WELL, YEAH. I MEAN, THERE'S NO ONE ELSE AROUND.

AS IF YOU WERE THAT COOL AROUND DEATH!
TYLER! DON'T BE RUDE!

WELL--I WAS CONCUSSED, AT THE VERY LEAST!

ALSO, HAVE YOU MET DEATH? HE'S, LIKE, A HUGE DORK. ***BUT*** ANYWAY...

YOU SHOULDN'T BE ABLE TO SEE ME.
BUT I CAN.

AND WHY'S THAT? THAT'S NOT RIGHT!
I'M, *UH*, I DON'T KNOW. SORRY??

THERE MUST BE A REASON YOU CAN SEE ME... ARE YOU SPECIAL?
MY MOM SEEMS TO THINK SO.
GOOD ENOUGH FOR ME.

I CAME FOR YOUR SOUL, BUT INSTEAD FOUND SOME UNTAPPED POTENTIAL... SO I'M OPENING A CROSSROADS FOR YOU. EITHER JOIN ME AS A GRIM REAPER, OR JOIN OTHER MORTALS IN THE DIRT. IT'S YOUR CHOICE.
UHH...!

THE NOT-DYING OPTION SOUNDS BEST TO ME.

AND THAT'S HOW I BECAME A GRIM REAPER!!
WHOA...

AND HOW CHARLIE BECAME A VAMPIRE, I GUESS.
IT IS TRUE.

DID YOU KNOW THAT?
IT FELT RUDE TO ASK!!

HEY, KIM...
HEY, YOU!

YOU KNOW HOW I WAS LIKE, VAMPIRES ARE GREAT! LET'S GO TO VAMPIRE ISLAND! OH BOY, ADVENTURE!!
A-HUH.

AND YOU WERE REUNITED WITH YOUR FRIEND! YOUR, *UH,* ***BEST*** FRIEND!
YEAH!

THIS HAS ALL BEEN A LOT TO TAKE IN AND I WOULD VERY MUCH LIKE TO GO HOME NOW AND NEVER RETURN.
HUH?

WE JUST GOT HERE, THOUGH!
MHM, WE'VE BEEN HERE FOR A COUPLE OF HOURS NOW... YOU JUST GOT BACK.
ALSO, BEHIND THAT DOOR THERE'S A WHOLE MESS OF VAMPIRES THAT WANT TO EAT ME AND TYLER.
IT'S, LIKE, A WHOLE THING.
WHAT DO YOU MEAN A WHOLE MESS OF VAMPIRES THAT WANT TO EAT YOU? WHAT DID I MISS?
LOOK, I'LL EXPLAIN WHEN WE GET--
AFT RO
OH, C'MON...!

CHARLIE, CHARLIE, CHARLIE...

...THE THING ABOUT BEING IMMORTAL, IS THAT OUR GRUDGES LIVE FOREVER...

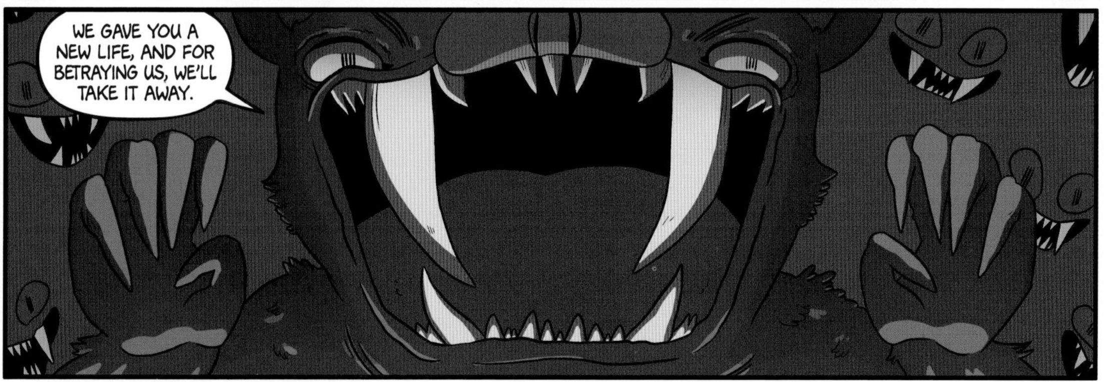
WE GAVE YOU A NEW LIFE, AND FOR BETRAYING US, WE'LL TAKE IT AWAY.

HELP! CHARLIE'S FAINTED!!

THEY'RE NOT THE ONLY ONE...

WHAT'S THAT... SMELL?

HI, SORRY, EXCUSE ME--
--I HAVE ONE HUNDRED GARLIC PIZZAS HERE FOR A CHARLIE?
Y'ALL, UH, HAVING A PARTY OR SOMETHING, HUH?
WHAT IS HAPPENING...?
AS IF THAT PLAN WORKED!!
QUICK, GET US OUTTA HERE!
THIS IS KIND OF WEIRD AND I MIGHT CALL THE POLICE...
Y'ALL ARE GONNA PAY ME BEFORE LEAVING, RIGHT?
NOT AGAIN...

WHAT JUST HAPPENED?!
YOU MISS STUFF WHEN YOU'RE AT WORK ALL THE TIME--
HEY, GUYS?

CHARLIE DOESN'T LOOK TOO GOOD.

GUYS...?

I DON'T WANT TO BE AT WORK ALL THE TIME!
THEN WE NEED TO DO SOMETHING ABOUT THAT.
AAAAAAAH!

BUT WHAT CAN WE DO?
GUYS!!

CHARLIE LOOKS BAD. REAL BAD!!

GARLIC IS SO TOXIC TO VAMPIRES, THIS PLAN WAS TOO DANGEROUS!
CHARLIE MUST'VE BEEN DESPERATE TO GET OUT.
MUST BE AWFUL BEING A VAMPIRE HUNTER TURNED VAMPIRE...
I DON'T KNOW WHAT TO DO! I DON'T KNOW HOW TO FIX THIS!!
IF GARLIC IS BAD, WHAT IF WE GAVE CHARLIE SOMETHING GOOD?
RESTORE THE BALANCE!! BUT WHAT'S GOOD FOR A VAMPIRE?
COUGH COUGH
BLOOD.

CHAPTER THREE

HEY, LET ME AND TYLER FIGURE THIS OUT--GO TAKE A BREATHER, WE'VE GOT THIS.

ARE YOU SURE? ONLY IF YOU'RE SURE--OH GOSH THIS IS **A LOT**.

ALRIGHTY, CHARLIE--

--CONSIDER ME YOUR PERSONAL BLOOD BANK, 'COS I AM GONNA HOOK YOU UP!!

EEEEEEEEEEEEE!

I MEAN, WITH BLOOD THAT IS *NOT MINE!*

AAAAAAAH.

LET'S FIGURE OUT NON-HUMAN SOURCES. HOW ABOUT ANIMAL BLOOD?
I GUESS.
NOOOOOOO!

FINE, WHAT IF WE ROBBED A BLOOD BANK?
ALSO BAD.
I NEED BLOOD NOW...!

WHAT DO YOU RECOMMEND, THEN? LET CHARLIE DRINK MY BLOOD?!
STEALING IS WRONG, BECKA!
PWEASE...
UH, GUYS?

WHAT?
UHH!!

I HAVE TO GO TO WORK.

AAAAAH!
UM.

AAAAAAAH!

...BECKA?

AAAAAAAAAAAHHH!!

BECKA!
AAAH!
KARATE!!!

...
HUFF!

I CAN'T DEAL WITH A VAMPIRE AND A GRIM REAPER RIGHT NOW!!
TYLER! YOU'RE ON CHARLIE DUTY!
KIM! YOU'RE WITH ME.
NOW OPEN UP A PORTAL TO SOME BLOODY STEAKS OR SOMETHING!!
LIKE, TO A RESTAURANT?
DO IT!
AAH AAH, OKAY!!
WILL THIS HELP?
YES!
MENU

TABLE FOR TWO?
PLEASE.
MENU

FOLLOW ME.

MENU
MENU

HERE YOU ARE.
TH- THANKS.
MENU

MENU
MEAT $$$
MORE MEAT $$
SUPER RAW MEAT
BASICALLY ALIVE MEAT

A PILE OF YOUR BLOODIEST STEAKS, PLEASE.
EXCELLENT CHOICE.
$

AND WHAT MAY I GET FOR YOU?
MENU
UHHHHH!

DON'T SUPPOSE YOU HAVE ANY VEGAN OPTIONS, DO YOU?
MENU
NO.
JUST A WATER THEN, THANK YOU!!

SO NOW THAT WE'RE ALONE, LET'S JUST REWIND FOR A SECOND.

"YOU CAN'T DEAL WITH A GRIM REAPER RIGHT NOW"? THAT WAS PRETTY RUDE OF YOU!
WELL, YEAH!!

SORRY BUT NOT SORRY FOR BEING BRASH BACK THERE, BUT WE HAD A DYING VAMPIRE SITUATION ON OUR HANDS! AND--

--I KNOW YOU'RE WORKING FOR DEATH! THE CONSEQUENCES ARE UNCLEAR! WE BROKE THE RULES AND NOW YOU HAVE TO WORK OVERTIME--

--BUT THEY'RE WORKING YOU TO DEATH, AND I NEVER SEE YOU ANYMORE!! I'M GRUMPY ABOUT IT! SO MAYBE I WAS TOTALLY RUDE IN THE HEAT OF THE MOMENT, BUT THE SITUATION BLOWS!!

SIGH I GET IT. I'M MAD TOO, BUT WHAT CAN I DO?

HOLD THAT THOUGHT!

I FEEL LIKE WE TOTALLY JUST CHANGED TRACK HERE--WHAT ARE YOU SCHEMING?
YOU SAID "I," BUT WHAT ABOUT "WE"?

MAGICAL GIRL TRANSFORMATION INTO...
...BUSINESS BABE!

'SUP.

...WHAT IS GOING ON?

WHAT IF *WE* TACKLE THIS PROBLEM TOGETHER? LET ME HELP YOU GET BETTER WORK HOURS! I'LL TALK TO THOSE BONEHEADS AND THEN WE CAN GET BACK TO SMOOCHIN'!

SOUNDS GOOD, BUT FIRST... SINCE WHEN HAVE YOU OWNED A SUIT?

I WORKED AN OFFICE JOB BEFORE THE BAKERY. WEIRDLY SIMILAR AMOUNTS OF CAKE, THOUGH.
YOU SHOULD LOSE THE TIE.

UM, THAT'S THE BEST PART, THOUGH!! LOOK AT THESE DOGS, KIM!
LOOK AT THESE BUSINESS PUPS, KIM!!

THEY'VE GOT LITTLE BRIEFCASES, KIM.
ALL RIGHT, OKAY...! AW, THEY'RE READY TO CLOSE DEALS.

YOU'RE NOT, THOUGH. GET CHANGED INTO THESE.

THOSE CLOTHES SMELL LIKE GARLIC.
AW, JEEZ, YOU'RE RIGHT!!

MAGICAL GIRL TRANSFORMATION INTO--

--A BUSINESS CUTIE!!
BECKA!
OKAY, WE'RE READY TO GO NOW.

YOU READY TO CONFRONT YOUR BOSS?
UMMM...

YEAH!!

IF YOU'RE NERVOUS, I'LL TOTALLY DO ALL THE TALKING?
OH YES, PLEASE!!

KIM?! WHAT ARE YOU DOING HERE?!

MY CLIENT IS HERE TO TALK ABOUT HER WORK CONTRACT.
WHAT?!

WHAT IS THERE TO TALK ABOUT?
I'M SORRY, BUT THAT IS BETWEEN MY CLIENT AND HUMAN RESOURCES. PLEASE DIRECT US TO YOUR HR PERSON.

EMPLOYEES MUST WASH UP AFTER THEMSELVES
YEAH, WE DON'T HAVE THAT.
WHAT?! THAT'S UNACCEPTABLE! A BIG ORGANISATION LIKE YOURS WITHOUT AN HR DEPARTMENT?!

I MEAN... THIS IS THE UNDERWORLD, AKA, ***HELL***.
I'M SAD ABOUT IT TOO!

WELL, JUST TAKE US TO THE GRIM REAPER IN CHARGE, THEN!!

WELL, THAT MIGHT BE A BIT TRICKY.
...

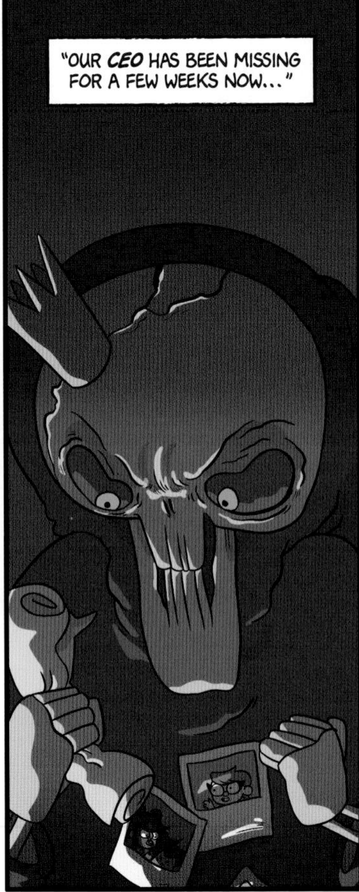
"OUR ***CEO*** HAS BEEN MISSING FOR A FEW WEEKS NOW..."

MEANWHILE...
KIM MUST BE STOPPED!!

WHEN I INTRODUCED HER TO THE BOARD, THEY WERE HESITANT, BUT I INSISTED! I TOOK A CHANCE ON HER, AND FOR WHAT?

EVER SINCE HER GAL PAL OR WHATEVER CAME ON THE SCENE, SHE'S DISOBEYED ME! EMBARRASSED ME! MADE ME LOOK THE FOOL...

SHE'S POWERFUL... BUT I CAN'T AND WON'T FORGET WHAT KIM AND HER FRIEND HAVE DONE TO ME ANYTIME SOON.

BACK IN THE UNDERWORLD.
I HAVE NO IDEA WHERE HE IS!
WHO'S IN CHARGE, THEN?!
#1 SPOOK

WE'VE BEEN TAKING IT IN TURNS.

I'M IN CHARGE TODAY!! JUST IN TIME FOR KIM TO DO ALL MY LAUNDRY AGAIN!!

THAT'S NOT GRIM REAPER WORK!
IT IS WHEN I'M IN CHARGE!!
BONK
THEY TOLD US TO SET YOU THE WORST JOBS... HE'S REALLY ANGRY WITH YOU AT THE MOMENT.

LOOK, I KNOW WE'VE BEEN HARD ON YOU LATELY...

I ASSUME THAT'S, *UH,* WHY YOU'RE HERE?
YEP!

WE JUST GOTTA DO WHAT HE SAYS! HE'S THE BIG BOSS IN CHARGE!

HE SIGNS OUR PAYCHECKS!
I'M SAVING FOR A BEACH HOUSE.

BUT YOU KNOW THAT IT'S WRONG! LOOK HOW SAD YOU'RE MAKING KIM WITH ALL THE SCUT WORK!

LOOK AT HER!!

UHH...

LOOK AT US!!

SORRY KIM, BUT I REALLY WANT THAT BEACH HOUSE.
BAH!
BUT HE'S NOT EVEN HERE! HE WON'T KNOW IF YOU LET UP ON BEING TOTAL JERKS TO KIM!
HE'S NOT HERE, BUT HE SEES EVERYTHING-- THAT'S WHY HE'S IN CHARGE!
A POWERFUL FORCE THAT RULES OVER BOTH LIFE AND DEATH! IT'S A HUGE AND STRESSFUL RESPONSIBILITY, AND MAYBE THAT'S WHY HE'S SO, *UH,* "QUIRKY."
BUT YOU DON'T MESS WITH POWER LIKE THAT! THE CEO CAN SEE AND HEAR EVERYTHING, AND THAT'S WHY HE'S OUR BOSS.
AND THAT'S WHY YOU'RE ON LAUNDRY DUTY.
SORRRRRYYY

QUIRKY IS A WEIRD WAY TO PHRASE "OUT OF CONTROL, TOTALLY UNFAIR JERK HEAD"!!

KEEP IT DOWN AND JUST FOLLOW THE RULES!
M-MAYBE...

WE ALL DO AND WE'VE GOT AN EASY LIFE! YOU COULD TOO!!
WE'RE GETTING NOWHERE WITH THESE LOW-LEVEL BONEHEADS--WE NEED TO TALK TO THE BONEHEAD IN CHARGE!

I DO THINK MR. BONES OVER THERE AGREES WITH US, BUT HE'S TOO SCARED TO ADMIT IT...

'COS HIS BIG BOSS HEARS ALL!
??

YOUR BOSS IS A BIG SMELLY NERD!!
GASP!
KIM! WHAT ARE YOU DOING?!
I'M TRYING TO LURE THE CEO OUT! IF I'M MEAN ENOUGH, HE MIGHT TRY TO CONFRONT US, AND THEN WE CAN CONFRONT HIM!!
OH!! I'LL HELP!

HEY, BIG BOSS ! YOU'RE A TOTAL NERD! A REAL !
AND THAT'S WHY YOUR MUM DOESN'T LOVE YOU ANY MORE!!

HOW WAS THAT?
TOO MUCH!! I SAID BE MEAN, NOT ATOMIC!
OH! I'M NOT USED TO BEING MEAN!! MEAN IS NOT MY THING AT ALL!! I FEEL AWFUL!

DON'T--IT LOOKS LIKE IT WORKED!
OOH.

YOU KNOW WHAT? I THINK I CAN TAKE IT FROM HERE...

TAKING A STAND CAN BE TOUGH, BUT I'M ONE TOUGH COOKIE!
THANKS FOR THE HELP, BECKA.

I'M PROUD OF YOU! TAKE MY SUITCASE FOR ULTIMATE BUSINESS SASS, HOPEFULLY IT'LL POWER YOU UP AS YOU TELL YOUR BOSS OFF!
THANK YOU, BECKA!

WHAT'S INSIDE?
OH NO, WAIT--

I FORGOT TO TAKE OUT MY OLD LUNCH FROM MY LAST SHIFT. WHICH WAS... A VERY LONG TIME AGO.
UMM.
JUST, UM, FORGET ABOUT THAT AND GO GET 'EM!!

KIM AND FRIEND! YOU'RE SUCH JERKS!

SORRY TO HAVE BEEN SO CRUEL, BUT I NEEDED TO GET YOU HERE! TO TALK FACE-TO-FACE WITH ME!

EXCUSE ME?
HOURS, REGULATIONS, LIMITS--A CHAT LONG OVERDUE!

NO!

BUT I'VE GOT A BRIEFCASE... I'M BUSINESS READY?

YOU'VE TALKED ENOUGH.

I'M DONE WITH YOU TALKING! WITH YOU DISOBEYING ME! NOT FULFILLING ORDERS! MAKING ME LOOK FOOLISH-- NO MORE!

I'M DONE WITH YOU, KIM.

KIM!!

WHOA, LET'S, UH, TAKE IT EASY NOW...

YOU HAD THE CHANCE TO TAKE IT EASY, TIME AND TIME AGAIN WHEN I GAVE YOU ORDERS--BUT YOU IGNORED THEM.
DID WHAT YOU WANTED TO DO AT MY EXPENSE.

NO MORE!

OH HECK, OH HECK, OH HECK!
SO THAT'S WHERE HE'S BEEN HANGING OUT... HUH.
THE SECOND LEVEL OF HELL.

WHY AREN'T YOU GUYS FREAKING OUT?!
LIKE, IT'S KIM...

...SHE CAN TAKE CARE OF HERSELF.
I'M NOT SURE, SHE'S IN BAD COMPANY.

WHAT DO YOU MEAN??
NEVERMIND HIM--

BUT WHAT I MEAN IS ALTHOUGH WE ALL KNOW HOW TOUGH KIM IS, SHE MIGHT BE IN TROUBLE RIGHT NOW.

THAT SECOND LEVEL OF HELL SHE'S BEEN DRAGGED INTO IS A NIGHTMARE REALM, AT BEST.

THAT LEVEL BREAKS THE MINDS OF EVEN THE MOST POWERFUL GRIM REAPERS, WHICH WOULD EXPLAIN A LOT...
WE HAVE TO SAVE HER!!

THE ONLY THING I'M SAVING IS MY MONEY. FOR A SWEET AS HECK BEACH HOUSE.

BUT, *UH,* LOOK. MAYBE WE CAN HELP FROM AFAR? IF YOU DON'T TELL ANYONE??

YOU CAN BORROW THIS SCYTHE--TEMPORARILY!! IT'LL EVEN THE PLAYING FIELD A LITTLE.

AND, LOOK, IF YOU MANAGE TO TAKE OUT THE CEO WHILE YOU'RE SAVING KIM, THAT'D BE NEAT!

BUT YOU DIDN'T HEAR THAT FROM ME!! OKAY?!

THIS FALL IS TOO HIGH, YOU'LL NEED TO PORTAL DOWN.
I HAVE A QUICK PIT STOP TO MAKE FIRST.

HERE IS THE BILL.
THANKS...

DOES BEING A VAMPIRE PAY WELL? BECAUSE I CANNOT AFFORD THIS.
I USUALLY BITE AND DASH. WANT ME TO DO THAT NOW?

OH, KIM'S HERE--MAYBE SHE CAN LEND US SOME OF HER "GHOUL CASH."

HEY, YOU'RE NOT KIM! YOU'RE BECKA? WITH A SCYTHE?!
KIM'S BEEN KIDNAPPED, WE NEED TO SAVE HER!!

SOUNDS LIKE WE NEED TO LEAVE RIGHT AWAY AND NOT WAIT AROUND TO PAY THIS BILL!

DIDN'T YOU SAY STEALING IS WRONG EARLIER?

NO TIME TO TALK ABOUT MORALS, WE'VE GOT A GOTH TO SAVE!!

YOU'RE RIGHT, LET'S GO!
NOOO, PAY THE BILL!!
NOT AGAIN...

CHAPTER FOUR

YOU'VE GOT A PLAN, RIGHT?
UM, YEAH.
WE'RE JUST GONNA SCOOT ON OVER TO THE SECOND LEVEL OF HELL (AKA THE NIGHTMARE REALM), WE'LL HEROICALLY RESCUE KIM FROM THAT BONEHEAD, AND THEN WE'LL SCOOT ON BACK HOME!
IT'S GONNA BE SO EASY! NO BIG DEAL!!
...I'M HAPPY YOU'RE SO CONFIDENT.
WHY WOULDN'T I BE?

OH HECK, BRACE YOURSELVES!
I CAN'T SEE ANYTHING!

OOF!
FWOMP

TYLER! CHARLIE! WHERE ARE YOU?!

I'M RIGHT HERE, YOU BOOB.
OH, THANK GOSH!!

COULDN'T YOU PORTAL US CLOSER TO THE FLOOR, MAYBE?
I'VE NEVER USED ONE OF THESE-- THESE STICKS, BEFORE!
KIM MAKES IT LOOK SO EASY...

CAN YOU SEE ANYTHING THROUGH THIS THICK FOG?! MORE IMPORTANTLY, CAN YOU SEE ANYONE... WHERE'S CHARLIE?
UM...

I THOUGHT THE SECOND LEVEL OF HELL WOULD BE BRIGHTER... MORE FLAMES AND LIGHT, INSTEAD OF ALL THIS SPOOKY MIST.

THEY'RE PROBABLY NOT TOO FAR, THOUGH! WE LANDED CLOSE TOGETHER!

CHARLIE'S NOT CURSED LIKE ME TO BE FOREVER MAGNETISED TO YOUR AURA OF DRAMA.
AW, THAT'S A MEAN GOOF, TYLER.

YOU'RE DRAWN TO ME BECAUSE I HAVE A FUN AND HAPPY AURA THAT'S DELIGHTFUL TO BE AROUND!

AND NOT BECAUSE YOU'VE BEEN CURSED BY A WITCH OR SOMETHING TO BE FOREVER AT MY SIDE, RIGHT...?
RIGHT?

JUST TO CONFIRM-- YOU DO KNOW WITCHES DON'T EXIST?

BUT THEY MIGHT!! VAMPIRES EXIST! KIM EXISTS!!
SO PROBABLY WITCHES AND FRIENDSHIP CURSES, TOO!!

...I NEVER THOUGHT OF THAT.
AAAAAH!

BECKA, I HAVE **NOT** BEEN CURSED TO FOREVER HANG OUT WITH YOU!! AND EVEN IF I HAD, JOKE'S ON THEM 'COS YOU **ARE** A FUN PERSON AND HAPPY WHATEVER-YOU-SAID TO BE AROUND.
OH... GOOD.

I THINK THERE'S SOMETHING UP WITH THIS FOG... IT'S MAKING ME FEEL GROUCHY AND ON EDGE, I'M SORRY...
MMM, I FEEL IT TOO. I GUESS THIS WASN'T GOING TO BE THE CHEERIEST PLACE...

THEN IT'S DECIDED! THE LESS TIME WE SPEND HERE, THE BETTER! LET'S FIND CHARLIE, RESCUE KIM, AND GO!!

YOU KNOW WHERE WE'RE GOING, RIGHT? YOU SAID YOU HAD A PLAN, YEAH? BECKA...?

HEY, HOP ON MY BACK. LIKE, RIGHT NOW.
OH!

SO I CAN SEE OVER THIS FOG AND FIND CHARLIE? THAT'S A GREAT IDEA!
OH, YEAH, THAT'S TOTALLY... TOTALLY THE ONLY REASON, *MMHMM.*

NOTHING TO DO WITH YOUR INTENSE PHOBIA OF BUGS AND THE LARGE AMOUNT OF THEM CRAWLING ALL AROUND US.
WHAT--

HUP!
WHAT?!

SO I GUESS IT WASN'T HYPERBOLE AND THIS IS *LITERALLY* A NIGHTMARE REALM!
YOU DON'T SAY!

ARE YOU SCARED OF ANYTHING ELSE? I CAN HANDLE BUGS, BUT IT'S GOOD TO HAVE A HEADS UP!
M-ME? WHAT ABOUT YOU?!

I'M NOT AFRAID OF ANYTHING!

I'M COOL LIKE THAT.

I THOUGHT YOU WERE AFRAID OF BIRDS.
WHAT? I AM ***NOT!!***

OH WAIT, I REMEMBER NOW.
REMEMBER WHAT?

AH.
YOU STILL COOL?
NO.

IT'S SO CUTE! I WANNA PET IT.
AAAH AAAAAH AAAH AAAAAH!
WAIT A SECOND...
...IT'S MADE OF BUGS!
AAAAAAH!!
I THOUGHT YOU SAID THIS WOULD BE EASY?!
I THOUGHT WRONG!!
BORK! BORK! BORK!
BECKA, WATCH OUT!
FOR WHAT, MORE GHOULS?!
FWOMP

WHAT THE...?
BECKA!
C'MON! GET IN HERE!!
BORK
BORK
BORK
BORK
Candyworld

LOOK AT THIS PLACE! LOOK AT ALL THIS CANDY!!
MAYBE THE NIGHTMARE REALM ISN'T ALL SO BAD--
NO WAIT, THAT CAN'T BE RIGHT.
DON'T TOUCH ANYTHING!!
DON'T WHAT NOW?
OH!
OHH!!

THIS DOESN'T MAKE ANY SENSE!!
BUT EVERYTHING WAS CUTE A SECOND AGO!!
NIGHTMARE REALM!
NIGHTMARE REALM!
NIGHTMARE REALM?
NIGHTMARE REALM!!
HEY, I JUST HAD AN INTERESTING THOUGHT. ACTUALLY, HECK THIS.
TYLER!
WE'RE IN TOO DEEP!
KIM NEEDS US!
WE'RE LITERALLY COVERED IN BLOOD!
WE HAVE TO FIND CHARLIE!

I HAAAAATE THIS!!
...ME TOO.

FINE! WE'LL SAVE EVERYONE FIRST, AND THEN GO HOME. BUT I'M GOING TO BE GRUMPY THE WHOLE TIME, OKAY?!
THAT'S GOOD WITH ME.
SLURP

SLURP
SLURP
IT'S NOT ALWAYS LIKE THIS, Y'KNOW. THE MONSTERS AND THE DRAMA AND THE SHOPS-THAT-LOOK-LIKE-CANDY-STORES-BUT-ACTUALLY-TURN-OUT-TO-BE-LITERAL-BLOODY-HELLHOLES...

...SOMETIMES THERE'S BEAUTIFUL MOUNTAIN PICNICS, AFTER-HOURS SNEAKY MUSEUM TOURS, AND A WHOLE TON OF HOLDING HANDS WITH A REAL CUTIE!
SLURP
SLURP
SLURP

AND THEN OTHER TIMES HER BOSS IS A COMPLETE CRETIN WHO KIDNAPS HER, WHICH LEADS US TO A VERY SCARY RESCUE MISSION!! I'M SORRY YOU'RE EXPERIENCING THE LATTER--
SLURP
SLURP
SLURP
SLURP

TYLER?
SLURP
SLURP
SLURP
SLURP
SLURP
WE HAVE COMPANY.

I THINK THERE'S A BACK ENTRANCE... WE CAN SNEAK PAST THIS CREEP.

LET'S TAKE IT SLOW, AND--

--BECKA?
SOB!

I REALLY WANTED YOU TO LIKE KIM, BUT NOW WE'RE GONNA GET EATEN BY A MONSTER!! AND YOU CAN'T LIKE KIM IF YOU'RE *MONSTER FOOD!*
W-WHAT? ***NO!!*** BECKA!

WE'RE ***NOT*** BECOMING MONSTER FOOD TODAY!! AND I WILL TOLERATE KIM AND ***MAYBE EVEN*** GROW TO LIKE HER ONCE WE RESCUE HER FROM THIS HELLSCAPE, AND ARE IN A MORE CHILL AND BETTER GETTING-TO-KNOW-HER ENVIRONMENT, OKAY?!
WE'RE GONNA BE ***OKAY!***

...WHAT'S THAT FACE FOR?

I GOT REALLY WRAPPED UP IN THE MOMENT.
IT'S OKAY, IT WAS NICE.

Y'KNOW, IF WE'RE MONSTER FOOD, WE DON'T HAVE TO PAY BACK OUR STUDENT LOANS.
YOU ALWAYS LOOK ON THE BRIGHT SIDE OF LIFE.
THE BRIGHT SIDE OF... DEATH?
HEH, UGH... YEAH.

GUYS? IS THAT YOU?

OH MY GOSH, IT IS!! I HAVE SUCH BAD BAT-VISION...

CHARLIE?!

IT ME!!

DID YOU THINK I WAS GOING TO EAT YOU AGAIN? THAT'S STILL TOTALLY RUDE, YOU KNOW.
WE'RE NOT MONSTER FOOD TONIGHT!!
YOU'RE OKAY!!

I LOST YOU GUYS, AND AT FIRST I WAS LIKE: *UGH,* THIS ***SUCKS!!*** THIS PLACE TOTALLY BLOWS--

--BUT THEN I FOUND ALL THIS BLOOD! JUST LYING AROUND, HOW WILD IS THAT?! I'M TOTALLY BACK ON TOP OF MY GAME NOW!

ONE PERSON'S NIGHTMARE REALM IS ANOTHER PERSON'S BLOOD HAVEN, I GUESS!
AH, THAT CLASSIC SAYING!!
WHERE'S KIM? HAVEN'T YOU GUYS SAVED HER YET? THAT'S WHAT WE CAME HERE TO DO, RIGHT?

WE GOT HELD UP BY A PRETTY NASTY... *UH*... BUG DOG??

BUG DOG? DOG MADE OF BUGS?
ATE IT.

DANG, CHARLIE'S SO COOL...
IT'S NOT WELL-DOCUMENTED, BUT VAMPIRES REALLY DO LOVE A GOOD BUG EVERY NOW AND AGAIN.

HOW DID YOU FIND US?
WELL, I WAS REALLY FOLLOWING THE SCENT OF BLOOD.
YOU GUYS WERE A LUCKY COINCIDENCE!

SEE, I'M LIKE A SHARK. OR MAYBE LIKE A BASSET HOUND?
I WOULD'VE GONE WITH "BAT."
I HAVE A KEEN SENSE OF SMELL!! IF I GET A WHIFF OF SOMETHING, I CAN HUNT IT DOWN!

OH! OH!! I KNOW HOW TO FIND KIM!!
KIM'S WEARING MY SPARE BUSINESS SHIRT--

IF YOU SMELL THE ONE I'M WEARING, COULD YOU TRACK HER DOWN, TOO?

HMM...

SSSNIIIIIIFFFFF
OH! HA HA, UM.

THAT WAS ODDLY NOT THE WEIRDEST THING THAT'S HAPPENED TODAY.
I'VE GOT HER SCENT!! SHE'S NOT FAR!

LET'S GO RESCUE KIM!!

eware the dog
o cold callers please
HOME sweet Home
SHE'S IN THERE!

WHAT'S GOING ON?!
TWO BLOBS ARE DOING... SOMETHING!!
MOVE IT.
OKEYDOKE.
FLUMP
AAAAAAAHHH!
IS THAT A GOOD OR BAD SOUND?
UM.
THE GRIM REAPER HAS KIM TRAPPED IN HIS GROSS OLD HOUSE!!
WE GOTTA GET HER OUTTA THERE!
THE DOOR'S LOCKED.
USE YOUR SCYTHE...
...TO MAKE A PORTAL. BUT THIS WORKS TOO, I GUESS.
KRAK
KIM!!

WE'RE HERE TO RESCUE YOU!!
WHAAAAAA!
RESCUE YOU?
WOOO!
STOMP HAT NERD!
OH BOY.
STEP AWAY FROM MY GIRLFRIEND!!
YAAAAAAAH!
YOU CAME ALL THIS WAY TO RESCUE ME?
WELL, YEAH!! NOBODY DRAGS YOU TO THE SECOND LAYER OF HELL AND GETS AWAY WITH IT ON MY WATCH!
OH MY GOSH...

I LITERALLY HAVE SOMEONE IN MY LIFE WHO WILL GO THROUGH HELL AND BACK FOR ME.
WELL, LIKE, IT'S NO BIG DEAL, REALLY... I'D, LIKE, TOTALLY DO IT AGAIN!

NAH, LET'S JUST GET OUTTA HERE.

GET A ROOM!!
HEY, COULD YOU GUYS DO THAT, LIKE, ELSEWHERE?! MAYBE?

OH YEAH... WE SHOULD CONTINUE THIS SMOOCH SOMEWHERE ELSE.
WHAT? NO!!

THIS JERK KIDNAPPED YOU! I THINK WE SHOULD STAND ON HIM FOR AT LEAST FIVE MORE MINUTES!!
NOOOOOOO!

WHAAAAA?!
IT'S OKAY-- WE ACTUALLY MADE UP. ME AND THE CEO ARE ALL GOOD NOW.

THE KIDNAPPING TOOK A WHILE, WHICH ACTUALLY GAVE US TIME TO TALK THINGS OUT.
YOU CAN'T DRAG ME DOWN HERE JUST 'COS YOU'RE MAD AT ME!!
I THINK I CAN AND I AM!
WHY ARE YOU DOING THIS?! YOU'VE GOT IT OUT FOR ME, AND IT'S MESSED UP!
IF YOU JUST OBEYED ME AND LET BECKA DIE, LIKE I HAD ORDERED YOU TO--
I COULDN'T KILL BECKA, SHE'S MY GIRLFRIEND--AND SURELY THAT COUNTS AS CONFLICT OF INTEREST?!
OOH, SHE IS? WELL, GOOD FOR YOU.
LOOK, WHAT IF I HAD TOLD YOU TO REAP YOUR SIGNIFICANT OTHER'S SOUL--
I DON'T HAVE ONE.
OH. WHAT ABOUT YOUR BEST FRIEND?
NOPE...
YOUR MOM?
STILL NO.
...YOUR DOG?
OL' BONEY MALONEY?!
no cold callers please
YEAH!!
NOOOO!!
OKAY, FINE! NO MORE PERSONAL REAPINGS--
OR LAUNDRY!
...
C'MON!!
OKAY, OKAY!!
BUT NO MORE DISOBEDIENCE.
WITHIN REASON.
DEAL.
...
ARE YOU HUNGRY? IT'S A LONG TRIP BACK, EVEN BY PORTAL.
I COULD EAT.

AND THEN WE MADE CUPCAKES!
EVEN THOUGH YOU STOOD ON ME, I'LL STILL LET YOU HAVE ONE.

SO... YOU DIDN'T NEED RESCUING AFTER ALL?
I APPRECIATE THE GESTURE! NOT MANY PEOPLE, IF ANY, WOULD DO WHAT YOU ALL DID FOR ME!

AW, MAN... I WAS GONNA KICK BUTT FOR YOU! KICK IT SO HARD AND SO RIGHT, AND IT WAS GONNA BE REALLY COOL.

I COULD RAISE THE DEAD AGAIN IF YOU LIKE?
OH! ACTUALLY, NO, THIS IS FINE AND GOOD! HEY, KIM, SHOULD WE LEAVE?
YES!

THEN LET'S GOOOO!
WOOOO!
WAIT, WHEN DID YOU GET A SCYTHE?!

EVERYTHING IS RESOLVED AND WE ARE AWESOME!!
WOO!
WELL, NOT *EVERYTHING*...

I STILL NEED A BETTER BLOOD SUPPLY! AND I KNOW WE HAVEN'T KNOWN EACH OTHER LONG, BUT... I'D BE HONOURED IF YOU HELPED ME ON THIS MISSION, TYLER!
M-ME? WELL, SURE!! OF COURSE!

THEN THAT SETTLES IT--LET'S GO ROB VAMPIRE ISLAND OF *ALL ITS BLOOD!*
WAIT, WHAT?!

SHOULD WE INTERVENE? I'M TOUCHED THAT TYLER CAME DOWN TO THE HORRIBLE DEPTHS OF HELL TO SAVE ME--SHOULD I RETURN THE FAVOUR?
NAAAH... OUR BEST FRIENDS SHOULD PROBABLY SPEND SOME TIME TOGETHER.
MY *BEST* FRIEND!

HEY, YOU DO KNOW THAT GIRLFRIENDS AND BEST FRIENDS ARE WHOLE DIFFERENT THINGS, RIGHT?
SO IF CHARLIE IS YOUR BEST FRIEND, THEN I'M YOUR BEST...?

YOU'RE MY NUMBER ONE BEST *EVERYTHING*... JUST SO YOU KNOW! NO BIG DEAL!!
I'M YOUR NUMBER ONE?! YOU THINK I'M THE *BEST?*

CHARLIE IS IMPORTANT TO ME, BUT YOU'RE LIKE, IMPORTANT **AND** EXTREMELY CUTE? I REALLY, REALLY LIKE YOU, BECKA.
I REALLY, REALLY LIKE YOU, TOO. YOU'RE VERY LIKEABLE FOR A GRIM REAPER, KIM REAPER.
OH, GOSH!
SO, I GUESS NOW WE'VE FINALLY GOT SOME TIME TOGETHER, AND YOU BEING THE VERY BEST AND ALL, YOU SHOULD CHOOSE WHAT WE--
OH...!! I CAN GET BEHIND THIS.
VAMPIRE TEEN DRAMA
BED COOKIE?
COOKIES
WHERE DID YOU GET THOSE?
COOKIES
DRAMA
END

ILLUSTRATION BY KATY FARINA

BONUS MATERIAL!

KIM & BECKA CHARACTER SHEETS

I changed up Kim's design between *Grim Beginnings* and *Vampire Island*--most notably, with the haircut. I wanted to show that some time had passed since the last arc, but also I had admittedly gotten tired of her old haircut. Short hair, big fringe is a cute new look, okay!!

Becka's design doesn't change much between the two arcs--her outfit is a little spookier, but that's only because you can't marathon *Vampire Teen Drama* without dressing accordingly!

Becka's ties are inspired by my Dad's work ties. They all had cartoon prints on them (and they were all kind of awful, sorry if you're reading this, Dad!).

CHARLIE & TYLER CHARACTER SHEETS

Charlie is influenced by a song titled "Charlie" by Allison Crutchfield. It's a song that does not mention pronouns, but does mention biting necks. If you skipped to the bonus content and haven't read the comic yet, spoilers!! Charlie is a non-binary vampire. They're also very sweet and they own a cardigan I wish I personally had.

Teen Charlie wears a pin with a very goofy vampire face and a cross through the middle. This is an inside joke (was an inside joke?) between me and my partner--he is forever drawing that same goofy vampire face in all my sketchbooks and on the corner of all my digital comic files when he thinks I'm not looking.

I had written the full script before sketching up these character sheets, and only then did I realize Tyler only gets one outfit throughout this story (if you don't count the vampire cape!!). It's a good thing he looks great in it!

MAKING THE COMIC

When writing a script, I'll break the story down into main plot points, and then start thumbnailing the pages. Thumbnails tend to be a little loose and help me figure out character expressions/layout for later, and definitely do not require me to actually draw a room full of proper vampires--that's a treat for future me at the pencilling stage!

YOU'LL HAVE TO EXCUSE THEM, THEY'RE NEW BLOOD.
I MEAN, **NO BLOOD!** WHATSOEVER!!
I ONLY JUST BIT THEM LAST WEEK, ***HA HA***. YOU KNOW HOW IT IS!
VAMPIRES ARE NO FUN.
HEY, YOU PROBABLY DON'T WANT TO DRINK THAT--
IT'S PROBABLY BLOOD.
BLEEEEEUUUGH!!

COVER DEVELOPMENT

When sketching up the cover ideas, I hadn't figured out Kim's new hair cut or Charlie's design yet! With the first issue, we thought it'd be fun for it to mirror the first issue of *Kim Reaper: Grim Beginnings*. Instead of skulls, I got to draw a lot of cute and round bats! I don't think there are small piles of blue furry bats on the real Vampire Island, but there definitely SHOULD be.

This was definitely my favourite unused cover, and it was probably the most nonsensical! Maybe Kim and Becka will return to the Underworld and there will be a story where they both obtain briefcases overflowing with money and I'll be able to use this cover, but only time will tell.

TWILIGHT-INSPIRED COVER

For BookExpo 2018, we did a *Kim Reaper* sample book for people to read! We decided it'd be fun to do a spoof on the *Twilight* movie poster for the cover.

VALENTINES

To celebrate the release of the first *Kim Reaper* book, I drew these valentines that people could download! We donated all the proceeds to True Colors Fund, which works to end homelessness among LGBT+ youth.

SARAH GRALEY

is a UK-based comic artist and writer, living with four cats and one cat-like boy. When she's not working on comics about part-time grim reapers and cuties, she's probably working on other comics about other cuties! She did that RICK AND MORTY™ series (LIL' POOPY SUPERSTAR) that one time, and also does a diary comic called OUR SUPER ADVENTURE. You can check those out and more at www.sarahgraley.com!